1

Bond, Michael
    Olga carries on.   Illus. by Hans Helweg.
Hastings House [1977]
    127 p.   illus.

I. Title

5

OLGA CARRIES ON

Olga Carries On

MICHAEL BOND

ILLUSTRATED BY HANS HELWEG

J
C. J

HASTINGS HOUSE, *Publishers*
NEW YORK

First published in the United States of America 1977
by Hastings House, Publishers.

Originally published in Great Britain by Puffin Books.

Copyright © 1976 by Michael Bond

Illustrations Copyright © 1976 by Hans Helweg

Library of Congress Cataloging in Publication Data

Bond, Michael.   Olga carries on.

SUMMARY: Olga, the guinea pig, meets new challenges as she
fights a fire and sets a trap for an uninvited guest.
   [1. Guinea pigs—Fiction]   I. Helweg, Hans.
II. Title.
PZ7.B63680j   [Fic]   77-8710
ISBN 0-8038-5380-7

Printed in the United States of America
Children's Catalog 6/22/10 P

CONTENTS

CHAPTER ONE

Olga's Present

Olga da Polga was suffering from 'mixed feelings'.
That is to say, one half of her was feeling reasonably
pleased with life, the other half of her was feeling
quite the opposite.

The fact of the matter was her family had gone
away.

Of course, it had its good side; most things do if
you look hard enough. Since they had been born her
three children had grown and grown, so that just
lately her hutch had become very crowded indeed.

But when she thought of the weeks she'd spent
bringing them up; the number of times she'd . . . well,
not exactly 'gone without', but awaited her turn at
the feeding bowl, words failed her.

And what upset her most of all was the way it had happened; suddenly, without so much as a 'please', or a 'do you mind', or even a 'thank you very much' afterwards.

Karen Sawdust and her father had arrived outside her house soon after breakfast one morning carrying a cardboard box, and before she'd had time to gather her wits about her the children had been lifted out, the door slammed shut again and she'd found herself all alone in the world.

What with all the squeaking and shrieking which had gone on at the time, any explanations were completely lost.

And none of her friends were of much help either. As soon as the coast was clear and the sound of Mr Sawdust's car had died away, they came out of their various hiding places and gathered round in order to hear what was wrong.

'Is that all?' said Graham, the tortoise, when Olga had finished her tale of woe. 'I thought something terrible had happened.'

'I expect they've been given away,' said Noel, the cat. 'That's what usually happens to unwanted families.'

Olga's jaw dropped. 'Given away?' she repeated, hardly able to believe her ears. '*Unwanted?*'

'Think yourself lucky,' broke in Fangio, the hedgehog. 'At least it means they've probably gone to a good home. Not like hedgehogs – left to fend for themselves, *and* as likely as not get run over the very first time they try to cross a road on their own.'

'Or drowned,' said Noel. 'That's what happens to kittens sometimes. I could tell you a few tales.'

Olga gave a shiver. 'I'd rather not hear them, thank you very much,' she squeaked.

Noel sniffed as he turned to go. 'I've never heard so much fuss being made over nothing,' he said.

But Olga had suddenly begun to remember snatches of conversation she'd heard that morning. Remarks that had passed unnoticed during the heat of the moment, and which were now flooding back.

For instance, she was sure Karen Sawdust had said she would bring something back with her. Yes, that was it, she'd said that when she returned she would bring a present!

Olga liked presents and she grew more and more excited at the thought.

'I wouldn't go yet if I were you!' she called.

The others stopped in their tracks.

'I may,' said Olga vaguely, 'have something for you soon.'

Noel looked at her. 'Something for *us*?' he repeated. 'What sort of something?'

'You'll have to wait and see,' said Olga mysteriously. 'But I'm sure it will be very nice. Karen Sawdust promised she would bring a present back with her.'

'Why are *we* getting one?' asked Noel suspiciously. 'They haven't taken anything away from us.'

'Not yet,' said Fangio ominously.

'I'm all right,' said Graham. 'They can't take anything away from me. I haven't got anything to take. And if they try I shall go inside my shell and I shan't come out again.'

'You'll all be getting a present,' said Olga patiently, 'because I shall be sharing mine.'

'At least,' she added, 'I shall be sharing it with those who are still here.'

'Do you mean to say,' grumbled Noel, 'that we've

got to hang around here all the morning listening to you complaining?'

'Complaining?' repeated Olga indignantly. 'You'd complain if you'd just had your own flesh and fur taken from you . . . it's very lonely without them.'

Noel, who secretly knew when he was beaten, stretched out lazily on top of the coal bunker near Olga's hutch and closed his eyes. It was as good a way as any of passing a warm, sunny morning.

'The thing is,' began Olga, as she gave the matter some more thought, 'I'm sure my family won't have been passed on to just anyone. After all, they must be very valuable.'

'Valuable?' Noel opened his eyes and looked at her scornfully. 'How do you make that out?'

'Well, I don't want to boast,' said Olga, 'but I mean to say . . . look who their mother was.' She preened her whiskers in the reflection from her water bowl.

'I cost twenty-two and a half new pence when I was new, and that was ages ago. Mr and Mrs Sawdust are always saying how things are getting more and more expensive all the time. Even the price of my oats keeps going up, and I eat lots of those, so goodness knows what I must be worth now.

'I mean,' she added, warming to her subject, 'it's not like cats. You said yourself they often drown kittens . . .'

Noel looked at her in amazement. For someone who didn't want to boast Olga was doing remarkably well.

'If I'm worth ten times as much as I was,' she continued, 'there's no knowing what they'll get for my children.'

Noel made a noise which was halfway between a sniff and a snort and then closed his eyes again, but Graham and Fangio began to look more and more impressed.

'Well, if I'm to have a present, I'd like a THIS WAY UP sign,' announced Graham, getting in first. 'I've always wanted one of those. People keep on picking me up and turning me over. I once saw a sign on the side of a box,' he went on dreamily. 'It took me all the morning to work it out because it had been put on upside down – but that's what it said – THIS WAY UP.'

'I'd like a bowl of bread and milk,' said Fangio hungrily. 'A great big one. A *bottomless* one.'

Graham considered this for a while. 'If it didn't have a bottom,' he said at last, 'all the milk would run out.'

'I don't mean *that* sort of bottomless,' said Fangio. 'I mean one that went on and on with no end.' He made a loud sucking noise. 'It needn't even be a bowl – it could be a hole in the ground, and the more you eat the more there is . . .'

Olga rustled her hay impatiently. 'I can't promise what it will be,' she said. 'You'll have to wait and see.'

As it happened the words had hardly left her mouth when there was a click from the side gate and Karen Sawdust came into view. She was carrying a small handbag, and as she drew near Olga's heart missed a beat. The big moment had arrived. What *could* be in store for her?

If Karen Sawdust noticed three other pairs of eyes watching her every movement she showed no sign.

'Poor Olga,' she said, as she opened the door. 'I'm sorry we had to take your family away from you without any warning, but there really wasn't room in your hutch for *four*. It was high time we did something about it.

'Anyway, they've all gone to a good home with a friend of mine. As I couldn't really ask her to pay anything for them, I did a swop instead.' She opened her handbag and took out a small piece of cardboard.

14

'My friend's father has a special camera that takes pictures while you wait, and he let me take one of your family in their new house.'

Olga watched in astonishment as Karen Sawdust took some sticky tape and fixed the piece of cardboard to the wall of her dining-room.

She blinked, and then she blinked again – just to make sure. For there, gazing back at her, were three very familiar faces.

Karen Sawdust closed the door again and fastened the catch. 'Whatever else you do,' she warned, 'don't chew the edges. It's the only picture we took and there'll never be another.'

There was a moment's silence as she went away, and then as the kitchen door shut the hub-bub broke out.

'I'm hungry!' wailed Fangio. 'It's thinking about all that bread and milk.'

'I'm going!' called Graham, 'before anyone picks me up and turns me over.'

'A *swop*!' exclaimed Noel bitterly. 'Who wants a picture of a lot of guinea-pigs?'

Olga drew herself up to her full height. '*I* do,' she said, with as much dignity as she could muster. 'And they're not just any old guinea-pigs. They happen to be *my* family. It's quite the nicest present I've ever had.

'You're welcome to share it with me,' she called. 'You can come and see it whenever you like.'

But the others had disappeared.

Olga gave a sigh. Really, there was no accounting for some tastes.

She lay back and studied her present with care. She would miss her children – there was no denying the fact – but they had to go out into the world on their own at some time, and their new owners sounded very nice and kind. In a way, she had the best of both worlds; she could still see her family and yet she hadn't the bother of looking after them. It seemed a very good arrangement.

'I expect it was the only thing Karen Sawdust

could do,' she announced, in case Noel, Fangio and Graham were still within earshot. 'After all, some things in this world are so valuable you just can't buy them – and my family happens to be one of them!'

CHAPTER TWO
Olga's Tallest Tale

One day Olga made a discovery. She discovered she was able to speak French. True, she could only say one word, and it wasn't a very long one at that; but as Karen Sawdust explained, it was more than a lot of human beings managed to learn in a whole lifetime.

Olga made her discovery quite by chance.

Early that morning Karen Sawdust and some of her friends came out into the garden in order to do something called 'rehearsing a play', and Olga was put in her special run so that she could watch what was happening and enjoy a late breakfast at the same time.

At first Olga spent more time watching the 'goings-on' on the lawn than she did eating the grass itself, but when she found the play had to do with 'The Wars of the Roses' she soon lost interest.

Olga knew all about the Wars of the Roses. They took place all through the summer, whenever Mr Sawdust came into the garden. In fact, as far as she could make out, Mr Sawdust spent more time battling with his roses than he did over anything else. If he wasn't cutting bits off the ends he was attacking them with something called a spray gun. Sometimes he fought battles against green flies; at other times he fought battles against black flies; and Olga had no doubt that if there had been any pink or blue flies on the roses Mr Sawdust would have found a spray for those as well.

Then there was some nasty white stuff called mildew, and something even worse called black spot. In fact, so many things seemed to go wrong with Mr Sawdust's roses Olga often wondered why he bothered to keep them at all. They were much more trouble than they were worth. It wasn't as if they did anything useful, for according to Fangio and Graham they weren't even nice to eat, and Noel was always grumbling about the sharp thorns they had all the way up their stems.

Another thing Olga didn't like about roses was the fact that often, if Mr Sawdust did his spraying on a day when the wind was blowing in the wrong direction, she wasn't allowed on the lawn for days at a time in case it made her ill.

Given her way, Olga would have had one really big War of the Roses and finished them all off for good. Giving a loud squeak of disgust, she turned her back on the proceedings and began tucking into the grass for all she was worth. There was no knowing if Karen Sawdust and her friends mightn't take it into their heads to do some spraying as well.

As it happened Olga's squeak was much louder than she had meant it to be, and it made the others stop what they were doing and look round at her in surprise.

'Did you hear that?' cried Karen Sawdust. 'Olga was speaking French! How about giving her a part in the play?'

'I don't see what the French have to do with the Wars of the Roses,' said one of her friends. 'It all happened in England.'

'But it was *after* the soldiers had got back from France that it happened,' insisted Karen Sawdust. 'They started fighting amongst themselves.' She picked up a stick and laid it on the grass. 'The bit between here and Olga's run can be the English Channel. Olga's run can be France. And Olga herself can look after it and make sure the fighting doesn't spread beyond the shores of England.'

They all crowded round the run, and feeling that something was expected of her, Olga lifted up her head and gave another loud squeak.

'There you are!' cried Karen Sawdust triumphantly. 'She said yes!'

'What a beautiful accent!' exclaimed someone else. And dissolving into gales of laughter, they all ran off again and went on with their play.

Olga felt very pleased with herself. 'Fancy me being able to talk in a foreign language!' she thought. 'And not only talk it, but make myself understood as well!'

Olga couldn't wait to tell her friends, but the play went on and on, so she had to keep the news to herself for the time being.

It was a very noisy play. There were several boys taking part – some with white roses pinned to their jackets and others with red ones, and they spent their time running up and down the lawn waving wooden sticks called 'lances', and shouting at each other. Whenever they fell over – which was quite often – Karen Sawdust and her friends took it in turns to help them to their feet and give them something called 'first aid'.

It was all very strange, but Olga did her best to join in. Each time anyone came near her run she dashed round and round in circles, squeaking as hard as she could.

'I think you defended France very well,' said Karen Sawdust, when the play came to an end at last and she moved Olga's run to a new spot on the lawn. 'You deserve some fresh grass as a reward for all your bravery.'

Olga felt very pleased with herself and she decided she would have to try and speak French more often.

'*French*?' exclaimed Fangio when she told the others about her discovery later that morning. 'What's French?'

Olga sighed. It really was most difficult trying to explain even quite simple things sometimes. 'It's another Sawdust language,' she said. 'It's spoken by people who live in France. People who live in other countries speak other languages.'

'I don't see why people have to speak another language just because they live in a different country,' said Graham. 'Why can't they all speak the same language?'

'Anyway,' broke in Noel, 'how do you *know* they

speak a different language if you've never even been there?'

Olga took a deep breath. 'I know,' she said wildly, 'because one of my relations invented French. It was my great-great-great-uncle, Sir Lancelot da Polga.

'That's how I come to speak such good French my-self,' she added. 'Karen Sawdust said I do, and she should know.'

The others sat and digested this piece of informa-tion for a moment or two while they tried hard to think of a suitable reply.

It was Noel who broke the silence. 'If you're so good at French,' he said, 'how about telling us a story in it?'

'If I told you a story in French,' said Olga, 'you

wouldn't understand a word. But I'll tell you how it came about in ordinary language if you like.'

She looked round the garden for inspiration, thinking over the morning's happenings and putting them all together in her mind.

'It started,' she said, after she'd got her ideas sorted out, 'at the time of the Wars of the Roses. You see, the French people were frightened that the fighting might spread across the English Channel, so they planted lots and lots of rose bushes all along their shores to stop the English soldiers getting in. They put special stuff on the ground to make them grow quickly, and they sprayed the leaves every day to get rid of all the flies, just like Mr Sawdust does with his roses.

'In no time at all the roses became so thick and tall and prickly that no one, not even if they'd used the biggest pair of clippers in the world, could ever have entered France.

'The only trouble was, they made such a good job of it that when the war in England came to an end the French people found they couldn't get out of their own country.

'Of course they could hear voices on the other side of the hedges – lots of them: because people kept on crossing the Channel to pick the roses. You see after the war there weren't many left in England. But they couldn't see anybody, and they couldn't make themselves heard either.

'They tried calling out "Help!" as loud as they could, but it was no use, the hedge was much too thick; and there were far too many thorns for them to push their way through.

'They decided that the only way they would ever attract attention would be by tying a flag to the top of one of the rose bushes, but not even the tallest Frenchman standing on the largest ladder in all France could reach anywhere near it.

'Then just as they were giving up hope of ever being rescued, my great-great-great-uncle, Sir Lancelot da Polga, came on the scene, bringing with him a tiny basket which he and some of the other guinea-pigs had made out of bullrushes.

'In those days,' continued Olga, 'guinea-pigs were often called on in times of trouble because they were so good at thinking up ideas. They were also very brave and noble and . . .'

'Oh, do get on with it,' said Noel impatiently.

Olga fixed him with a beady eye. 'Uncle Lancelot's idea was a very simple one,' she said, 'and when he'd explained to the French people what he wanted they granted him his every wish.

'They called on their tallest soldier, mounted him on the largest horse they could find, and then tied the basket to the longest lance that anyone had ever seen.

'As Uncle Lancelot climbed into it and the soldier rode off to a point somewhere near the horizon you could have heard a blade of grass fall to the ground.

'When he reached his chosen point, the soldier turned his horse, lowered the lance and charged.

'They do say that even to this day the sound of horse's hooves brings people running from their houses.

'When he was within a stone's throw of the rose bushes he brought his horse to a halt in a cloud of dust, and Uncle Lancelot shot out of the basket like a bullet from a gun and flew through the air towards the topmost branch.

'As he clasped it, the crowd, which had been standing watching in silence, suddenly gave out a great cheer.

' "Can you see over the top?" they cried. "Tell us, can you see over the top?"

' "Yes!" Uncle Lancelot's voice echoed round the valley far below. "Yes! Yes! Yes!"

'And that,' said Olga, 'was how the French language came to be invented, and how my uncle came to be called Lancelot.'

She sank back on her haunches, nibbling absent-mindedly at a morsel of grass. Telling stories was very tiring work, and it had given her quite an appetite.

'Wait a minute,' said Noel thoughtfully. ' "Yes" isn't a foreign word. The Sawdust people say it all the time.'

'I've heard them,' broke in Fangio.

'Me too,' agreed Graham. 'I don't think very much of that as a story.'

Olga looked round carefully before replying. 'Well,' she whispered, 'the thing that no one knows – the thing that's never been told before . . . not until today, is that Uncle Lancelot didn't really say "yes".

'You see, when he landed on top of the rose bushes he caught his paws on some prickles. So what he really said was "Wheeeeeeeeeeeee".'

And to show what she meant Olga opened her mouth as wide as it would go, and gave voice to the loudest cry in the best possible accent she could manage. 'Wheeeeeeeee! Wheeeeeeeeeeeee! Wheeeeeeee-eeeeeeeee!

'From that moment on,' she continued, 'the word "wheeeeee" has always meant "yes" in French.

'Of course, other people came along afterwards and thought up more words. Once the idea caught on it was easy, and they thought it might be nice to have their own language. But it was really my great-great-great-uncle Lancelot who started it all . . . and we guinea-pigs have been able to say "yes" in French ever since. "Wheeeeeee!" '

Olga glanced round, but to her surprise her audience seemed to have vanished.

'How useful it is to know a foreign language,' she thought. 'Especially when you want to enjoy your lunch in peace. I must remember to practise it in case I ever need it again!'

CHAPTER THREE

Olga's Best Effort

One day, Olga was sitting in her outside run on the lawn, enjoying a quiet nibble in the sunshine, when she smelt a smell.

There was nothing very unusual about this. The Sawdust family's garden was full of smells. The roses, the flower-beds, the shrubs, the heather-filled banks, the vegetables, all gave off some kind of odour for those with a nose to smell it.

Even each different blade of grass had its own particular scent; not to mention the occasional dandelion or piece of clover – *when* she could find them.

Olga counted the days when she found a clover or

a dandelion leaf on the Sawdust family's lawn as 'lucky' ones indeed, for Mr Sawdust worked hard to keep the grass free from what he called 'weeds'.

Olga had never quite got used to these odd ways of the Sawdust people. She couldn't understand what made them like one plant and not another, and why they should want to destroy perfectly good eatable things simply because they didn't like the look of them. There was no accounting for tastes, but if she'd had her way all lawns would have a liberal sprinkling of all sorts of nice plants besides grass.

But the smell she could smell that morning had nothing to do with anything immediately nearby. It wasn't a fresh, spring smell; nor was it a dusty summery one; it was almost an autumn smell – yes, that was the best likeness she could think of. It was the kind of smell that usually heralded the coming of autumn, when bonfires made up of dead leaves and branches were lit in the general clean-up before winter set in.

Olga wondered for a while if she could smell the smell because she was in a different part of the garden. The Sawdust family had arrived home late that morning from what was known as 'Saturday shopping'. There had been a great deal of rushing about and talk of a snack lunch of egg and chips. Olga had been put on the front lawn for a change – it had to do with Mr Sawdust having sprayed his roses in the back garden once again – and then they had all disappeared into the house.

She looked around, but apart from the familiar stone-like shape of Graham asleep under some bushes, there wasn't a soul in sight. Noel had gone out early that morning and probably wouldn't be back until much later, and Fangio was doubtless hiding away somewhere until it was time for his evening bowl of bread and milk.

Olga returned to her nibbling, but for once her mind wasn't on it. The smell was getting stronger all the time and it began to bother her more and more. Her nose twitched, and try as she might she couldn't rid herself of the feeling that something was very wrong.

There was little wind, but what there was seemed to be blowing the smell in her direction. She turned round in order to see if there was anything going on behind her and suddenly became rooted to the spot.

Her eyes bulged and she stared through the wire mesh of her run, hardly able to believe she was seeing aright. For there, not a dozen run length's away, was a great column of black smoke billowing out of the Sawdust family's kitchen window.

Olga had seen smoke coming out of their kitchen window in the past – usually on mornings when Mr Sawdust did something called 'burning the toast'. But when that happened, he always opened the door and waved a newspaper to and fro to get rid of it. On this occasion there was no one around, and it was all much, much worse than anything she'd seen before.

'Wheeeeeeeeeeeee!' she shrieked.

'Wheeeeeeeeeeeeeee! Wheeeeeeeeeeeeeeee! Wheeeeeeeeeeeeeeeeeeee!

'Help! Fire!

'Wheeeeeeeeeeeeeeeeeeeeeeee! Do something!'

And she ran up and down her run calling out as loudly as she possibly could.

'Wheeeeeeeeee! Wheeeeeeeeeeeeeee!' If only she could get outside. She felt so helpless shut in behind her wire.

But the only effect her shouting had was to waken Graham. He stirred in his sleep, looked around drowsily for a moment or two, and then ambled slowly in her direction.

'Is anything the matter?' he asked as he drew near.

'Is anything the matter?' repeated Olga. '*Is any-*

thing the matter? Can't you *smell* what's the matter? There's only a fire, that's all! The Sawdust family's house is on fire and no one's doing a thing about it!'

She ran around her run several more times and then stopped in front of Graham again. 'You'll have to raise the alarm!' she exclaimed.

'*I* will?' Something about the way Olga was behaving began to infect even Graham and he looked quite worried. He gave a sniff. Now that she mentioned it he could smell an unusual sort of smell.

'How? Why? What? Where?' he cried.

'I don't know!' squeaked Olga. 'Find someone else! Find Noel . . . or Fangio . . . or anyone. But do *something*!'

'Leave it to me!' said Graham. 'I'll be as quick as I can.'

Olga gave a groan as he lumbered past. 'No, not *that* way,' she cried. 'Wheeeeeeeeeee! Wheeeeeeeeeeeeee! The fire's the other way!'

But Graham wasn't to be diverted.

With his head down he disappeared round the back of Olga's run, heading goodness knew where in the excitement of the moment.

Olga sank back on to her haunches and gave another despairing groan. Fancy! Of all the creatures to be left alone with at such a time it had to be Graham – the slowest one of all.

Suppose the whole house caught fire? And the trees, and the grass . . . she might be burnt alive and all her whiskers turned into umbrella handles. She'd

once got too near a candle on her birthday and had had a terrible fright when one of her whiskers had singed and rolled itself up into what Karen Sawdust called an umbrella handle. It was something she had never forgotten.

In her panic Olga began to dig at the grass. 'Wheeeeeeeeeeee!' she shrieked. 'Wheeeeeeeeeeeeeeee! Wheeeeeeeeeeeeeeeeeeeeeeeeeeeeee!'

Whether or not she would ever have tunnelled a way out was hard to say, but long before Olga had a chance to find out, things began to happen.

Karen Sawdust came running out of the house. Olga felt the run being lifted up, and then she was safely in warm hands and out of harm's way. After that so many things took place all at once it wasn't until much later that she could even begin to sort them out. All she could do was sit in her house and watch wide-eyed.

There were shouts and cries from the Sawdust family. More smoke – clouds and clouds of it. Flames, even, licking up the kitchen wall. Then there was the wailing of a siren; at first in the distance, but getting closer and closer all the time. Then more shouts, this time from lots of men in dark uniforms. And the pounding of feet, followed by mounds of white stuff like soap suds, which seemed to cover everything.

After that there was silence, followed by a very

poohy, pongy smell, much worse than anything that had gone before, but thankfully a much 'quieter' sort of smell – without the crackles and pops of the earlier one.

'We left a frying pan on the stove and forgot to turn off the gas,' explained Karen to one of her friends much later that day, as they cleaned Olga's house out. 'It caught fire while we were out of the room and then set light to Daddy's new wall panels!'

Olga took it all in. She knew about frying pans. She knew more about frying pans than she cared to remember, for she'd seen Mr Sawdust rush past her house with one all covered in flames. And she knew about Mr Sawdust's wall panels as well, for she'd had many an afternoon's nap spoiled by his hammering while he was putting them up.

Karen Sawdust looked very black. In fact all the Sawdust family looked black, for they had spent the rest of the day cleaning up the mess.

'Thank goodness Olga raised the alarm,' said Karen Sawdust to her friend. 'I don't know where we would be if she hadn't.'

She closed the door of Olga's hutch, and then looked through the wire mesh. 'I told the man in charge of the fire brigade and he said he thought you ought to have a medal, so . . .' She felt in a pocket of her jeans and took out a small, silvery object. 'I've made you a special one all to yourself. It's an O.B.E!'

'An O.B.Wheeeeeeeeeeeee!' squeaked Olga with excitement. She hadn't the slightest idea what it meant but it sounded very important.

'O.B.E.,' said Karen Sawdust, as she pinned the object on to the wire netting, 'is short for Order of the British Empire – or Olga's Best Effort – which-ever you prefer.'

Olga knew exactly which *she* preferred, and when Karen Sawdust went and fetched a large pile of dande-lion leaves and clover to make up for the lack of lunch earlier, she felt her day was complete.

Her mouth full of greenery, she gazed up at the medal long after Karen Sawdust and her friend had gone back indoors. One moment chewing rapidly, the next moment sitting stock still as if transfixed, she looked as if she could hardly believe her eyes.

The truth of the matter was she was longing to tell someone her good news, and there was just no one around.

Neither Noel nor Fangio had put in an appearance all day, and if the noise was anything to go by the Sawdust family were still busy with their cleaning operations. Anyway, they already knew about it. It was all most disappointing.

And then she heard a rustle in some nearby bushes.

It was Graham. But a very different Graham than the one she'd last seen that morning. His shell was covered with mud; his feet were black; and his eyes were red and rimmed with sweat. He looked in a truly dreadful state as he dragged himself slowly nearer and nearer.

'Am I too late?' he gasped. 'I went everywhere I could think of but I couldn't find anyone, and then I lost my way and . . .'

'Are you too late?' Olga gazed at him indignantly.

'Why, it's been ov . . .' She was about to launch into one of her best ever tales; all about her moment of glory and how she alone had saved the day; but she caught sight of Graham's eager face looking up at her and she paused.

Then she did a very noble thing.

'No,' she said firmly. 'You're not too late at all. In fact you're just in time. You're just in time to see our medal.'

'*Our* medal?' repeated Graham.

'Yes,' said Olga. 'It's an O.G.E. Some people get it wrong and call it an O.B.E., but it's not – it's an O.G.E. That means Olga and Graham's Effort.'

'Can you eat it?' asked Graham hopefully. 'I'm hungry.'

'No, you can't,' said Olga. 'And even if you could, it would be wrong. Medals are only given on very special occasions. But you *can* eat these . . .' And she carried the remains of her supper across her dining-room and began pushing it through the holes in the front door.

Graham blinked happily as it floated down and landed beside him. 'What a funny thing,' he said. 'I do believe it's raining dandelions.'

He started munching the greenery and then looked up. 'Wouldn't it be nice,' he added happily, 'if we could have an O.G.E. every day?'

CHAPTER FOUR

A Model Guinea-pig

Olga crouched in the middle of the Sawdust family's dining-room table and gazed around the room with a very superior look on her face indeed.

The curtains had been drawn; chairs taken away in order to make more space; and all kinds of strange objects – big, shiny things with wires hanging from them – had been brought in; all because of her.

It was most exciting, and when the door swung open and Noel strolled in to see what all the fuss was about she could hardly contain herself.

'Look at me!' she squeaked, as she ran round and round in circles. 'Wheeeeeeeeee! You'll never guess what's happening!'

But if she was expecting her words to have any effect on Noel she was disappointed. He took in the scene with one disdainful glance. 'It looks as if you're going to have your photograph taken,' he said, trying hard not to yawn.

'I should think you'd be a fiftieth of a second exposure at f8. Unless of course you keep running round and round in circles like that. If you do, they may have to change things – just to be on the safe side. Otherwise it will come out blurred.'

'f8,' repeated Olga. 'A fiftieth of a second exposure? What *are* you on about?'

'I was forgetting,' said Noel, in world-weary tones. 'You wouldn't know about these things. You've never had your photograph taken before. It's all to do with letting the right amount of light into the camera.

'Mind you, if Karen Sawdust's taking the picture she's got a camera with the places already marked. There's one for bright sunshine, and another for cloudy days, though I don't suppose there's anything marked "guinea-pigs" – there wouldn't be any call for it.'

'They're getting someone in specially to take *my* picture,' broke in Olga, trying to get a word in edgeways. 'And it's going to be in colour.'

'You mean there are other sorts?' asked Noel. 'What are they taking? Head and Shoulders?' He

looked Olga up and down. 'Oh, I'm sorry, I forgot –
you haven't really got any shoulders. Never mind, I
expect they'll find some way of doing it. After all,
it isn't as if you've got black fur like me.

'The trouble with black fur,' he continued, 'is that
it soaks up all the light. Mr Sawdust says he has to *pour*
the lights on sometimes and it all disappears – just
like water.'

'If you've got so much light inside you,' said Olga
crossly, 'why don't you show up when it's dark?'

Noel couldn't answer that one, and to Olga's
relief he stalked out of the room. She was glad to see
the back of him. Really, if he'd gone on much longer
it would have upset her whole morning.

But she soon forgot the interruption in the general
excitement as the rest of the family came back in and
started making ready for the big moment.

As she'd told Noel, her picture was being taken by a
friend of the family and it was needed for a SPECIAL
PURPOSE. Karen Sawdust had told her so while she
was giving her fur a brush that morning in order to
make sure it was all neat and tidy. 'You're the only
one who's just right for the purpose,' she'd said.

'Well,' thought Olga, 'it's quite understandable of
course. I mean, they must be fed up with looking at

47

pictures of cats. If you're going to take photographs at all it might as well be something worthwhile.'

And as the lights came on in all the shiny reflectors she turned to face the front. She'd never seen such bright lights before, not even in mid-summer, and for a moment or two they made her blink. In fact they were so bright she could hardly make out what was going on in the rest of the room. All she could see were vague, shadowy figures. But listening to what was being said she gathered they were busy doing something called focusing the camera.

'We shan't be long now,' said Karen Sawdust, as she came round in front of the lights and turned Olga so that she was sideways on. 'But we have to make sure you come out nice and clear.' And she put some dandelion leaves on the table to make certain Olga stayed where she'd been put.

Olga was a bit disappointed she was only having a sideways picture taken of her. She'd always considered her face was her best part. But she thought it over while she sat chewing the leaves, and decided it was probably the best way of getting all of her in.

However, as it turned out the Sawdust family's friend took not one, but lots and lots of photographs. Most of them were from the side, but there were

48

quite a few from different angles as well. Some from the front, some from the back, and one from right overhead. Then she took some measurements with a long piece of tape, and afterwards she even drew a life-size picture on a big sheet of white cardboard, which she then coloured with a special box of paints.

At last it was all over. The lady thanked Olga very much and said how good she had been; the lights were switched off; the curtains drawn back; and Olga was returned to her own house.

After so much time spent under the hot lights it seemed cold and dark; even – though Olga hardly liked to admit it – a trifle dingy. If it hadn't been for the fact that Karen Sawdust brought her out a special feed of oats she would have felt very miserable indeed.

'That's a present for being such a good model,' said Karen Sawdust as she filled the bowl.

'A model!' squeaked Olga. 'Wheeeeeeeeeeeeee!' And she lost no time in telling the others all about it.

'A model what?' asked Noel suspiciously.

'Er . . . a model guinea-pig,' said Olga lamely. 'I expect they want to stand one in the garden like a gnome.' Olga had once seen some plastic gnomes in someone's garden when she'd visited Boris at the sea-side.

'I don't like gnomes,' said Fangio darkly. 'I've seen some up the road. Nasty things. You can't tell what they're thinking.'

Olga had a sudden thought. 'Perhaps it's a statue,' she exclaimed. 'The Sawdust people are always putting statues up to remind them of famous deeds.'

'Famous deeds?' repeated Noel. 'What famous deeds have you ever done?'

'I was thinking,' said Olga, with as much dignity as she could manage, 'of what happened with the fire.

They might want to stand a statue of me in the front garden just to remind them.'

'Oh, *that*!' Noel suddenly lost interest and wandered away. He was still upset at having missed all the fun, and he was also tired of hearing the same old story retold so many times.

'Well, if it *is* a statue,' said Graham, 'I expect they'll want to do one of me as well. Perhaps I'd better go and wait by the back door just in case.'

Olga returned to her oats. 'I think,' she said, in her 'its-high-time-we-changed-the-subject' voice, 'we shall just have to wait and see.'

But as things turned out Olga had a very long time to wait before she heard any more news about her photograph. Several weeks went past, and she had almost forgotten about it when one morning Karen Sawdust arrived outside her house carrying a mysterious-looking brown paper parcel under her arm.

It was an unusually long parcel. Olga couldn't remember ever having seen such a long one before, and she watched eagerly while Karen Sawdust unwrapped the paper.

'What do you think of that?' asked Karen Sawdust, as she held up a long, furry object. 'Do you recognize yourself?'

'Do I recognize myself? Wheeeeeeeee . . . . . .!'
Olga started to squeak in surprise and then broke off
as the rest of the paper fell away and she stared at the
object in front of her.

She had never felt so disappointed by anything in
the whole of her life. Words failed her. There wasn't
a squeak in her entire vocabulary which could have
possibly expressed her feelings at that moment.

True enough the face wasn't bad: quite good
really. Not like the real thing, of course – the whiskers
were much too coarse – but then that wasn't really
surprising. And the rear end, as far as she could judge,
was reasonably true to life.

But as for the body . . . it was too long by miles.
Why, it was longer than her hutch. It was practically
as long as two hutches put together. How anyone
could possibly make such a mistake she couldn't begin
to think. There was only one thing to do in the circumstances. She would ignore it. That's what she

would do – ignore it. And she turned her back on it without so much as a further glance.

Karen Sawdust went back into the house. 'I don't think Olga liked it very much,' she heard her say to her mother.

'Never mind,' Mrs Sawdust's voice floated back. 'It's ideal for what we want. Just the right length.'

Olga pricked up her ears. 'Perhaps,' she thought, 'it's been made that long so that as many people as possible can see it. That's it . . . there probably aren't enough guinea-pigs to go round to please everybody, so that's what they've done.'

Olga felt better. She even began to wish she'd taken a longer look at the model of herself, whatever use the Sawdust people intended putting it to.

But it was Noel who finally solved the mystery. There was a bang from the pussy-flap later that evening as he came hurrying out.

'Here!' he called. 'You'll never guess what they're using your statue for.'

Olga looked at him suspiciously. There was something about the tone of Noel's voice, not to mention the look in his eye, which she didn't much care for. 'If I'll *never* guess,' she said, 'there's not very much point in my trying...'

'They've put it against the dining-room door to keep the draft out,' said Noel. 'I only found out because I tried to push the door open just now and there was this great long thing in the way. It gave me a fright, I can tell you.

'The Sawdust people are always worried about drafts. It's because they haven't got any fur. Their legs get cold and it makes them cross and . . .'

He looked up, but Olga had gone into her bedroom. She didn't want to hear another word.

'That's the very last time I let anyone take *my* photograph,' she thought. 'And if they do try I shall run round and round and round so fast there won't be a camera made that will ever, ever catch me!'

And with that she buried herself deep inside her hay to keep out the draught and went to sleep!

CHAPTER FIVE

A Mystery Solved

'Tell me again,' said Olga. 'Slowly, and from the very beginning.'

Noel stood up, curled his tail neatly round himself, and then settled down again.

'There's a guinea-pig trapped in a pipe down near the shops,' he said. 'We had to stop on the way to the vet this morning and I heard it calling out. It was still there on the way back, squeaking away like mad.'

'What was it saying?' asked Olga. 'It must have been saying *something*.'

Noel gave himself a quick lick. 'That's the funny thing,' he said. 'It wasn't really saying anything. I mean, it *sounded* like you – as if it needed oiling, but there was nothing that made any sense.'

'Then how do you know it wanted help?' asked Olga. 'It might be very happy where it is.'

'Because it only calls out when people get near,' said Noel. 'As soon as it sees a crowd of people it starts going "Wheeeee! Wheeeeeeeeee! Wheeeeeeeeeeee!"; and when they've gone again it stops, so it must be trying to attract their attention. If it was happy it would go on squeaking all the time.'

'Perhaps it's invented another foreign language?' suggested Graham. 'Like your great-great-great-uncle Lancelot.'

'But what makes you think it's trapped in a pipe?' persisted Olga, ignoring the interruption.

'Because I happen to have very good hearing,' said Noel. 'And I *know* that's where it's coming from.'

Olga sat back and considered the matter. She had to admit that although any list of Noel's good points would have been fairly short, the one thing he was good at was hearing things. Noel could hear a bird

clearing its throat at the other end of the garden, and
if he said the sound was coming from inside a pipe
then there could be no doubt that it was.

'Well,' she said at last. 'I don't know. I'd like to do
something to help, I really would. But without
knowing what it's saying I don't see what I can do.'

'We can't leave him there,' said Fangio. 'That's for
sure.'

'If only I could get out of my house,' said Olga. 'I'd go down there straight away. Nothing would keep me away. *Nothing.*'

Noel looked at her thoughtfully. 'I know one way you could get there,' he said.

Olga's jaw dropped. 'You *do*?' she exclaimed.

'You could get there the same way that I did,' said Noel. 'If you get yourself taken to the vet you're bound to go past. Mr and Mrs Sawdust always go that way. I should know. I've been enough times.'

In saying he frequently went to the vet, Noel was making the understatement of the year. There were occasions when it seemed as though he practically lived there, and Mr Sawdust was always grumbling about the bills. If he wasn't having injections for one thing he was being given tablets for something else. His present visit had to do with a fight he'd been in the previous night. No one knew who his opponent had been, and Noel himself was very vague about the whole affair, but he'd lost quite a lot of fur off one of his back legs and was really looking rather sorry for himself.

'I'm not getting into any fights,' said Olga firmly.

'It doesn't have to be a fight,' said Fangio. 'You could have an accident. Perhaps you could scratch yourself on one of the wire netting ends in your hutch.'

'There aren't any wire netting ends in my hutch,' replied Olga. 'Mr Sawdust was very careful when he made it.'

'You could let Noel give you a nip,' suggested Graham.

'Certainly not!' said Olga, before Noel had a chance to reply. She didn't like the way he'd suddenly started licking his lips, and she went back to her bowl of oats with the air of someone who'd declared the conversation at an end.

'If you're frightened of getting hurt,' said Noel, breaking the silence, 'there *is* one other way.'

Olga looked up at him suspiciously.

'You could stop eating,' said Noel. 'Mrs Sawdust is bound to think there's something wrong with you if you stop eating – she always does.'

'What a good idea!' said Fangio.

'If Olga stopped eating,' said Graham wisely, 'there *would* be something wrong with her.'

Olga, her mouth full of oats, gave him a withering look. 'I think it's a perfectly silly idea,' she said. 'If I stop eating I shan't have any strength left to do anything at all. I shall be no use whatsoever.'

'You don't need any strength to listen,' said Noel, pressing home his point. 'And you won't have to *do* anything except go without food long enough to get yourself taken to the vet. You can make up for it later. I bet once you start eating again you'll be given lots.'

'Dandelion leaves,' said Graham.

'And fresh clover,' added Fangio, encouragingly. 'I remember once when I was ill I had cream off the milk for days afterwards. I was sorry when I got better again.'

'I'll just finish off my breakfast,' said Olga casually, 'then I'll think about it. I can't think on an empty stomach.'

'You won't get taken to the vet on a full one,' said Graham bluntly. 'That's for sure.'

Olga began to look more and more gloomy. It was all very well for Graham to talk. Having a shell meant that no one would ever know what state his stomach was in.

'The sooner you start,' said Noel, 'the sooner you finish. Besides, think how *you* would feel trapped inside a pipe.'

Olga struggled with her conscience for a moment or two longer before finally giving in. And really, as

61

she sat back basking in the congratulations that followed she began to feel rather noble.

It was only when she returned and caught sight of her bowl of oats, still half-full from breakfast, that she began to wonder if she was doing the right thing after all.

'Don't worry,' said Noel, cheerfully. 'It won't take the Sawdust family more than a few days to see that something's wrong.'

'A few days!' Left on her own, Olga hardly knew what to do with herself. Never had her food bowl looked quite so tempting. And the closer she got to it the worse it became. In the end she could stand it no longer and she disappeared into her bedroom and lay down in the hay with her back to the world.

Even when Karen Sawdust came to see her later in the day she still didn't budge.

Instead, she sat listening to the familiar sound of the dustpan and brush as the floor of her dining-room was cleaned out. Then, to her relief, she heard Karen Sawdust call out to her mother. 'Olga hasn't eaten very much today,' she said. 'I hope there's nothing wrong with her.'

'Perhaps she's tired of oats,' called Mrs Sawdust through her kitchen window. 'It may be the warm weather. Try giving her more greenstuff.'

Olga groaned inwardly a few minutes later when Karen Sawdust returned carrying a pile of assorted tit-bits. Her nose twitched as she smelt the good smell of freshly picked grass, and dandelion leaves, and clover – all the things she liked best in the world. She was supposed to get them *after* she'd been to the vet, not before!

To make matters worse, Karen Sawdust seemed to be taking extra-special care over everything that evening. She emptied out the food bowl, washed it carefully, and then filled it to the brim with fresh oats. Even the water bowl had never looked quite so clean and sparkling before. Olga could see it all out of the corner of her eye. But even though the pile of greenstuff was placed temptingly outside her bedroom door, she steadfastly refused to take any notice.

'I hope you feel better in the morning,' said Karen Sawdust, as she shut her up for the night. 'If you don't we'll have to take you to the vet.'

Although in one way the words were like music to Olga's ears, in another sense they were no comfort at all, for 'tomorrow' was a long, long way away.

'If I feel like I do at the moment,' she thought, 'I may not even *be* here in the morning!'

But if that day had seemed long, the night was much worse. Sleep was a long time coming, and even when she did finally nod off it was only to dream of food and yet more food; all tantalizingly just out of her reach.

Really, she didn't know which was worse, dreaming about food or seeing the real thing and being unable to touch it.

To make matters worse Noel gave her no peace. His pussy-flap hardly stopped banging as he kept coming outside to make sure she was sticking to her bargain.

At long last dawn broke, and then – rather earlier than usual – Karen Sawdust came to see her.

'Poor Olga,' she said, when she saw the pile of

uneaten food. 'You *must* be feeling off-colour. I've never known you to leave your food for as long as this before.'

'And you won't ever again,' thought Olga. 'Not if I have my way. Not ever and ever again. If I go on like this I shall be so off-colour I shall be white all over.'

But to her dismay there was worse to come. Instead of taking her out of the house as she'd expected, Karen Sawdust went through the whole business of cleaning it out again and fetching still more fresh food and water. Really, it was unbearable. She couldn't stand it any more. Karen Sawdust had promised to take her to the vet the very next day and now, here she was, still sitting in her house surrounded by food.

'It's Sunday,' said Noel, when he came to see her again.

'Sunday?' repeated Olga. 'What do you mean, Sunday?'

'The vet doesn't open on Sundays,' said Noel. 'Except for very special cases. They'd forgotten about that.'

'I'm special!' squeaked Olga. 'I'm very special!'

'Well, they've decided to leave it until tomorrow,' said Noel. 'I heard them talking about it at breakfast this morning. Mr Sawdust thinks you've got plenty of fat to live on until then.'

'Plenty of *fat*?' Olga could hardly believe her ears. 'How does he know what I've got underneath my fur? Wheeeeeeee!' She tried to give a squeak of disgust, but words failed her.

How she got through the rest of that day and the following night Olga never did know. She had lots of visitors, and her food was changed several times, but by then she was feeling too weak and miserable to care. In fact, she'd almost forgotten the real reason for her fast, and it wasn't until she felt herself being picked up and placed into her travelling box that it all came back.

The thought put new life into her, and as they drove

off she had a quick nibble at the hay which had been put in the box to protect her from the jolting.

She felt the by-now-familiar swaying motion as Mr Sawdust drove the car up the short driveway and into the lane outside, then down the long, winding hill leading to the shops and the spot where Noel had said he'd heard the cries for help.

Olga braced herself as they turned into the main road, and sure enough, a moment later she felt herself plunge forward as they drew to a sudden halt.

This must be it. This must be the place where Noel said they always had to stop.

Straining her ears to the utmost, she pressed herself against a small airhole in the side of the box. She could hear the sound of other cars. A screeching of brakes as they, too, came to a halt. The sound of hurried footsteps, and of people talking. But there was no sign of a guinea-pig, only a high-pitched 'bleep, bleep, bleep'. In fact the 'bleeping' was so loud and urgent-sounding, Olga wondered how even Noel, with his keen sense of hearing, could possibly have heard anything as small and delicate as a guinea-pig's voice.

'I expect it's been without food for so long now,' though Olga, 'it's just like me. I don't suppose it has the strength to say anything.'

And then she pricked up her ears again as she heard the Sawdust family talking.

'This new pedestrian-crossing idea certainly seems to be working,' said Mr Sawdust.

'It's such a simple idea too,' agreed Mrs Sawdust. 'I mean all you do is press a button, the lights change, the traffic stops, and "bleep, bleep, bleep" . . .'

'Everybody starts hurrying,' broke in Karen Sawdust. 'It always makes me get a move on. I even saw Noel on it the other day. Goodness knows where he was off to.' She laughed. 'Perhaps he thought it was Olga calling out. It sounds rather like a guinea-pig. Wheeeeeee! Wheeeeeeee! Wheeeeee!'

'How strange,' said Mrs Sawdust, as there was a rustling at her side. 'Olga must think so too. Listen . . . she's joining in.'

'Perhaps she's feeling better,' said Mr Sawdust as the bleeping noise outside stopped and they moved on their way.

'Joining in?' repeated Olga.

'Feeling better?

'Wheeeeeeeeeeeeeeeeee!

'To think . . . I've been going without food all this time just for the sake of a . . . a . . . *pedestrian crossing*!

'Cats! Wheeeeeeeeeeeeee!'

And she dived into her hay and gobbled it down so fast that by the time they reached the vet there was hardly any left. And if it didn't entirely make up for all the food she'd been without over the past two days, at least it gave her more than enough energy to decide exactly what she would have to say to Noel when she got back home.

CHAPTER SIX

Some New Arrivals

One morning Noel tore out of the house in a state of great excitement. Or rather, to be more exact, the kitchen door suddenly shot open and he came flying out with his tail between his legs, uttering a yowl which caused all the other occupants of the garden to stop dead in the middle of whatever it was they happened to be doing.

As the door slammed shut again he skidded to a halt, slunk along the path for a couple of yards, then paused for a brief and highly unnecessary wash.

But even to the most casual observer it was clear he had something on his mind, and shortly afterwards, having recovered his dignity, he turned and strolled purposefully across the lawn towards the others.

'We've got some new arrivals!' he announced.

'Some new arrivals!'

'Who?'

'What?'

'Where?' Olga joined in the general excitement as the news sank in.

'They're called Fircone and Raisin,' said Noel, 'and I can't tell you *what* they are, but I know *where* they are. They're in Karen Sawdust's bedroom. The door was open when I went past just now and I saw them.'

Olga suddenly felt rather downcast. To have additions was bad enough, but to find out that they were being kept in Karen Sawdust's bedroom was rubbing salt into the wound. True enough, in the past, she'd often been taken there as a treat when her house was being cleaned out, or when the weather turned particularly cold – she could safely say she knew every nook and cranny, especially the best ones to hide in when it was time to go home again, but she had never, ever been invited to *live* there. It was all most un-settling. The very idea made the grass taste so funny she nearly stopped eating it.

Noel licked his lips. 'I thought perhaps they were a present for me,' he said hungrily, 'but I don't think they could have been. I wasn't even allowed a proper look. You should have heard the fuss that went on as soon as I put my head round the door.'

Noel had had his fill of investigating for the time being, and on the pretence of having better things to do he disappeared for the rest of that morning.

However, Karen Sawdust's room was on the ground floor, and several times during the next few days he managed to climb on to the outside window ledge without being noticed. In this way he gathered a lot of extra information, all of which he passed on to the others.

Gradually they found out what the new arrivals looked like. It seemed that Fircone and Raisin had golden brown fur, large eyes, and long tails – which they could be picked up by. They were very clean in their habits, and apart from tearing up bits of paper which they used for their bedding, hardly ever needed cleaning out. They had cost £1.20 and their favourite food was something called sunflower seeds, which came in a big, yellow packet. When they weren't eating these they spent a lot of their time sleeping.

'They don't *do* very much, do they?' said Olga, looking up from her feeding bowl one day. 'I mean, all they seem to do is eat and sleep.' And she went into her bedroom and lay down for a quick nap just to show her disapproval.

She was getting a bit fed up, not so much with Fircone and Raisin as with hearing Noel go on about them. Just lately he had talked of little else, and Graham and Fangio were more than eager to listen. Her position as story-teller-in-chief was in danger. Every time she opened her mouth to say something Noel was off again. If it wasn't about what Fircone and Raisin were actually doing, it was about where they were doing it.

If Noel was to be believed, their home was a very splendid affair indeed; painted dark blue, and full of every gadget and comfort you could think of.

There was an upstairs bedroom, reached by a sloping ramp, and on the ground floor there was a special tray which could be taken out without disturbing the occupants on the rare occasions when they needed cleaning out. There was a wheel which went round whenever Fircone or Raisin climbed inside it – Noel said it went so fast you could hardly see their legs move; and to cap the lot Mr Sawdust had made them a long wooden tunnel from a hollowed-out tree branch, which they could hide inside when they wanted to be alone. It made her own house seem quite drab by comparison.

But the unkindest cut of all came one morning when she overheard a conversation between the Sawdust family.

'Are you going to the pet shop this morning?' called Mrs Sawdust.

An answering 'yes' floated back from Karen Sawdust. 'I'm getting some food for Fircone and Raisin.'

'Well, don't forget Olga needs some more oats,' called Mrs Sawdust.

'I'll try not to!' came the answering cry.

'I'll try not to!' repeated Olga. '*I'll try not to*! Wheeeeeeeeeeeeeeeeee!'

Her squeak of disgust was so loud it was enough to

make any pet-shop owner within miles rush to line his counter with packets of oats, just to be on the safe side.

And then Noel made another discovery about Fircone and Raisin. It seemed that when they were upset, or cross about something, they made loud drumming noises with their back legs on the floor of their house.

Unfortunately for Noel this was something he didn't find out about until it was too late.

After days of hanging around outside Karen Sawdust's bedroom he slipped in there one morning while the Sawdust family had their backs turned, and hid under the bed. No one knew just what evil thoughts he had in the back of his mind, but his hour of triumph was short-lived.

The combined efforts of Fircone and Raisin drumming their feet on the side of the cage brought the Sawdust family running, and for the second time in a little over a week Noel came flying through the kitchen door. Only this time there was a difference. This time he hadn't escaped completely unharmed. Pausing in order to have his usual wash in times of trouble, he licked his paw, and when he took it away again the fur on the end had gone an ominous shade of red.

Someone or some*thing* had taken a bite out of the end of his nose!

Olga looked at it with interest. 'I shouldn't worry too much about licking it,' she said, trying hard to keep the note of satisfaction from her voice. 'I think it's going to rain soon. Anyway, fancy letting little things like that get the better of you. I *am* surprised!'

Noel arched his back. 'Little things?' he repeated stiffly. 'Did you say *little* things?'

Olga stared at him in surprise. Somehow, for no reason other than the sound of their names, she had always pictured Fircone and Raisin as being small. Certainly no larger than herself.

'How big *are* they then?' she asked.

Safe in the knowledge that he was the only one present who had actually seen them, Noel began to embroider his tale in the hope of regaining some of his lost prestige.

'I'm not saying how big they are,' he began, rubbing his nose again, 'but I wouldn't like to be any of you lot if they ever get out. They'd have you for breakfast for a start. Why, they've got whiskers as thick as the bars on their cage. And as for their teeth – they're like celery sticks, and sharp as needles. It's all those sunflower seeds they've been eating. It's made them grow and grow and grow. If you knew the struggle I had . . . I'll tell you all about it if you like . . .'

'No, thank you,' said Fangio hastily. 'I'm going.'

'Wait for me,' called Graham.

'If you really want to know how big they are,' called Noel, 'I'll try and show you.' He stared round the bottom half of the garden until his gaze lighted on an enormous rhododendron. 'Can you see that bush over there?' he asked.

But if Noel was expecting any reply from his audience he was disappointed. They were looking in completely the opposite direction, and a moment later he discovered the reason why.

'Noel,' said Karen Sawdust, as she placed a very small blue cage on the ground alongside Olga's run, 'you're a naughty cat. Fancy trying to frighten my gerbils like that. No wonder they bit the end of your nose. It serves you right and I hope it taught you a lesson. You ought to be ashamed of yourself.'

Encouraged by the sound of Karen Sawdust's voice, Fircone and Raisin came out from inside the pile of shredded paper in their bedroom and peered at the others. Then they ran down the ramp and clambered up the rails at the front of the cage, staring out inquisitively. They were scarcely bigger than a medium-sized carrot.

'Say hello to Olga, Fangio and Graham,' said Karen Sawdust.

Olga suddenly decided she liked the newcomers after all. Anyone who was so small and yet could stick up for himself and bite someone hundreds of times his own size must have some good in him. She decided to get in first.

'Wheeeeeeeeeee!' she squeaked. 'Welcome to the family.'

The squeak which Fircone and Raisin gave in return was very small and very high.

It was friendly, but there was definitely a note of warning to it. Noel, who'd been about to let his instincts get the better of him again, understood it only too well, and he promptly sat down for another wash.

Olga relaxed. She was a great believer in starting as you mean to go on, and it was perfectly clear that Fircone and Raisin felt the same way.

She turned to Noel. 'What was it you were saying about a bush?' she asked. And there was a warning note in her voice too.

Noel busied himself with his washing. 'Nothing,' he said meekly. 'I only asked if you could see it, that's all.'

CHAPTER SEVEN

Olga Writes a Poem

As the summer wore on, finding fresh grass for Olga
became more and more of a problem for the Sawdust
family. The weather had been warmer than usual,
with very little rain, so the grass in their garden was
soon used up. The lawn itself hardly grew at all, and
gradually they began to go further and further
afield in their search for fresh supplies.

Olga could usually tell at once where her grass

came from. If it was from a field then it was often quite eatable, but if it came from the side of a road – particularly a main road – then it tasted of what the Sawdust family called 'diesel fumes', and with no rain to wash it clean it could be most unpleasant. True, Karen Sawdust always apologized in advance for its state, but that didn't make it taste any better.

And then one day Olga had a nice surprise. Karen Sawdust arrived outside her house carrying a large plastic bag, which was full to the brim with some of the lushest and greenest-looking grass she had ever seen.

Olga's sensitive nose twitched as the front door swung open, and she uttered a loud 'Wheeeeeeeeee!' of approval. This was more like it! She could hardly contain herself.

'It's from Tennyson's Lane,' Karen Sawdust called out to her mother. 'There's masses and masses of it. I don't know why we haven't thought of going there before.'

'Well, Olga should be all right for a while then,' said Mr Sawdust thankfully. 'After all, it's National Trust – and that does mean no one can build on it.'

'What a sensible idea,' thought Olga, 'keeping grass in a National Trust especially for guinea-pigs.'

Not that she cared where the grass had come from; she was much too busy eating it. It really was the most delicious she had ever tasted, and while the rest of her house was being cleaned out she chewed happily away, hardly listening to what was being said.

But gradually she became aware that Karen Sawdust was talking. And not only talking, but talking in a very strange way. Olga usually understood most of the things Karen Sawdust said, and even if she didn't know what every word meant she could always put two and two together and make at least three – enough to get the general idea. This was partly because Karen Sawdust spoke very clearly, but also because she mostly talked about sensible things – like food and drink.

However, for once Olga couldn't make head or tail of what it was all about.

> '*See what a lovely shell,*' said Karen Sawdust.
> '*Small and pure as a pearl,*
> *Lying close to my foot,*
> *Frail, but a work divine,*
> *Made so fairly well*
> *With delicate spire and whorl,*

How exquisitely minute,
A miracle of design!'

Olga knew what shells were. The inside of Boris's castle at the sea-side had been decorated with shells. But even though she craned her neck as far as it would go she couldn't see any lying at Karen Sawdust's feet. It was all very odd. Unless she was standing on them it didn't make any sense at all.

Olga decided to go back to more important things, and she was still chewing away later that evening when Noel appeared. He was closely followed by Graham and Fangio, and all were ready and eager for their own suppers.

Noel looked enviously at Olga's house when he caught sight of some bits of grass sticking out through the side of her front door. He liked an occasional blade for medicinal purposes, and as he strolled past he reached up automatically to take one.

'I know where this came from,' he said after a moment's thought.

'So do I,' said Olga. 'It's from Tennis Lane.'

'Not Tennis Lane,' said Noel. 'Tenny*son*'s Lane. That's quite different. I go there sometimes when I'm out for a walk.'

Olga pricked up her ears. Although she was perfectly happy in her house, firmly believing that if she waited long enough all that mattered in the world would sooner or later come to *her*, she always liked to hear about the coming and goings of others. This was particularly so with Noel, because he was often away for such long periods, and came back looking so tired, she felt he must go to interesting places.

'Tennyson,' said Noel, 'was a poet.'

Olga paused. 'A poet?' she repeated. 'What's a poet?'

'A poet,' said Noel vaguely, 'is someone who says things in a funny way so that you don't know what they're on about in the middle, but the end bits always sound the same. Karen Sawdust reads poetry when she does her school homework – that's how I know. It goes on for ages and ages sometimes.'

'So that was it,' thought Olga. 'Poetry. Karen Sawdust must have been doing her homework poetry while she was cleaning me out.'

'This Tennyson,' continued Noel, 'was very famous and he used to live near here. He had a special spot where he walked when he was writing his poetry, so that's why they call it Tennyson's Lane.'

'I expect that's why Karen Sawdust went there

in the first place,' thought Olga. 'How very lucky!'

She stopped chewing. 'To think,' she said romantically, 'I may be eating the very same grass Tennyson once walked on.'

'Ugh!' Noel made a choking noise, for he was rather fussy about his food. 'I hadn't thought about that!'

But Olga was miles away. 'I would like to write a poem,' she said dreamily.

Fangio looked up from his bread and milk. 'Animals don't write poetry,' he said bluntly.

'I wrote my name in the sawdust once,' boasted Olga, 'and it was all jumbled up in the middle for a long time. But the ends were very good. I'm sure I could write some.'

The others waited in silence for a while, but if they were hoping for any sign of the rhymes they were unlucky. Olga simply carried on with her eating.

'I'll . . . er . . . I'll try and have something for you tomorrow morning,' she announced. 'I can't do it straight away. I'm really rather busy.

'Perhaps,' she added as an afterthought, 'we could all think of a poem and see which one is best.'

'Oh, I couldn't write a poem,' said Graham. 'I don't think I could do that.'

'Neither could I,' agreed Fangio. 'I wouldn't know how to start, and as for the middle and the end . . .'

'You don't know what you can do until you try,' said Olga grandly. And she disappeared into her bedroom for some peace and quiet while she set to work.

Olga stayed awake late that night, making marks in her sawdust, scratching them out again, adding some things and taking others away. But she had to admit she hadn't a single idea in her head, and the

more she tried the harder it seemed. It was all very well for Tennyson – he'd had a walk with lots of grass on it where he could write *his* poems, but all she had was her own two rooms, and by now her sawdust was in such a state it would need a lot of work with a brush and pan to put it right again.

'Oh, dust!' she exclaimed at last. 'Dust and mogeration!' And she went back into her bedroom, closing her eyes in the hope that if she went to sleep something or other would happen during the night without her having to do anything more about it.

Olga slept much longer than usual. It was already well into the following morning when she woke. Her hutch had been cleaned out and a breakfast of oats and a further supply of the new grass was waiting for her. All signs of her efforts at poetry writing had long since disappeared.

As she came out of her hay, blinking in the strong light, she discovered Noel, Fangio and Graham waiting outside her house.

Fircone and Raisin were there too. Their cage had been put on a table outside the Sawdust family's back door, so that they could enjoy the morning sunshine as well.

'There you are,' said Noel. 'We were wondering where you'd got to. How's your poem?'

'Poem?' repeated Olga. '*Poem?*' For a moment or two she wondered what on earth Noel was talking about, and then it all came back to her. 'Oh *that*,' she said carelessly. 'I didn't want to write too many in case I got so far ahead you never caught up. You can have more time if you like . . .'

'Don't worry,' broke in Fangio eagerly. 'I've done lots. I did them while I was having supper last night.'

'So have I,' said Graham. 'You were quite right. You don't know what you can do until you try.'

'How about this one?' said Fangio. 'It's all about a carrot.

> '*The goodness they hold,*
> *Makes you lively and bold.*'

'Mine is about a bumble bee,' said Graham.

'*A bumble bee,*
Is hard to see,
When you are not very well,
And you live in a shell!'

'*Cats,*' said Noel, trying to get a word in edgeways,
'*Don't wear hats.*'

'I've got another one,' exclaimed Fangio. 'I've
just remembered it.

'*Shrubbery*
Sometimes tastes rubbery!'

'I've done one about crossing a road,' called
Graham. 'It's a bit long, so I hope I get it right.

'*If I was a toad,*
I would hop over the road,

91

But as I'm not,
I don't go out a lot.'

'*Cats,*' said Noel,
'*Are good at catching rats.*'

'I've got another one,' said Fangio.

'*There are ants*
In the cucumber plants.'

'We've done one as well,' called Fircone and
Raisin. 'We did it between us.'

'*Sunflower seeds,*' said Fircone,
'*Are a bit like weeds.*'
'*We know,*' added Raisin,
'*Because we've watched them grow.*'

'There are some in the bit of ground outside Karen Sawdust's window,' he explained. 'I expect she dropped them there one day when she was cleaning us out, but we couldn't get all that in to a poem.'

'*I can't run very fast,*' broke in Graham,
'*So I'm always last.*'

His voice trailed away as he caught the look on Olga's face and mistook its meaning. 'I know they're not very good,' he said. 'But they're the best I could do in the time. I don't suppose they're half as good as yours.'

Olga stared from one to the other full of indignation. How *could* they come out with such things when she'd been sitting up most of the night and hadn't a thing to show for it?

'Wheeeeeeeee!' she squeaked in disgust, making up the first words that came into her head. 'Wheeeeeee! *Ombomstiggywoggles!* Wheeeeeee! Wheeeeeeeeeeee-eeee! Wheeeeeeeeeeeeeeeeeeeeeeeeeeee!'

Noel, Fangio, Graham, and Fircone and Raisin looked up at her admiringly.

'That's good,' said Fangio. 'That's very good. I like that.'

'The ends are the same,' agreed Graham. 'And the

middle doesn't make any sense at all. That's what I call a *real* poem.'

'I don't know how you thought of it,' said Noel grudgingly.

'Oh, it just came to me,' said Olga modestly.

She tried it out again. 'Wheeeeeeeeeee!' she squeaked. '*Ombomstiggywoggles* and Wheeeeeee! Wheeeeeeeeeeee! Wheeeeeeeeeeeeeeeeee!'

The more she said it the more she liked it. There was a very nice sound to it indeed. She was quite sure even Tennyson himself couldn't have done any better.

'How nice,' she thought, as the others went their separate ways and she was left to get on with her breakfast. 'How nice to think that Tennyson and I both like the same grass. I might never have thought of it otherwise!'

CHAPTER EIGHT

Olga Sets a Trap

Noel was in disgrace. And not just any old disgrace, but a really big one.

His troubles started when Mrs Sawdust came downstairs one morning and found the waste bucket lying on its side with its contents spread all over the kitchen floor. The very next day the remains of 'something' – no one ever did discover what – were found lying on the mat. Rugs had been disturbed, cupboard doors squeezed open, the larder raided; in fact one way and another whoever was responsible had been having a high old time.

Because he was the only one with a free run of the house during the night – able, because of his flap in the back door, to come and go as he pleased – the blame had fallen on Noel. He'd been threatened with all sorts of dire punishments – including being locked out for the night and having his pussy-flap boarded up.

Noel was very bitter about it all. 'I wouldn't mind if I'd done it,' he meeowed. 'I wouldn't mind at all then, but I didn't.'

'If you didn't,' said Olga one morning, after he'd been going on about it for rather longer than usual, 'then who did?'

'I've got my suspicions,' said Noel darkly. 'If you ask me it's "Stinker" Martin. He's found my flap and he uses it when I'm not there. I can tell by the smell.'

A wave of sympathy ran round his audience, and even those who had treated the matter fairly lightly up to that moment began to take a different view.

All the animals had their own territory, and poaching on anyone else's ground was very much frowned upon. It was the kind of thing to be expected from foxes and other lesser creatures who knew no better, but not from one of their own kind. However, they all agreed it was typical of 'Stinker' Martin.

'Stinker' lived a little way up the road, and although most of the time he kept himself very much to himself, there were times – when the moon was high, or he was feeling just plain bored – when he went on the prowl; and if that happened it was time to watch out, for he hadn't earned his name for nothing.

'Why don't you lie in wait for him?' suggested Olga. 'You could hide behind your flap and pounce on him when he's halfway through.'

'You'd be lucky,' said Noel gloomily. 'I can see *him* getting caught like that!'

'Perhaps if you're locked out,' said Graham, 'and it still happens, they'll see it wasn't you and . . .'

'If *I'm* locked out,' said Noel, 'then "Stinker"

Martin will be too – so they'll still think it's me. I tell you, I'm done for!' And with that he stalked off into the bushes, leaving the others to carry on the discussion without him.

'We must do something,' said Olga after a while.

'The thing is,' said Fangio, 'what?'

'Leave it to me,' said Olga grandly. 'I shall think of a plan. I shall call it MY PLAN. You'll see.'

Fangio looked up at her scornfully. 'What can *you* do,' he asked, 'shut up in your house all night?'

But Olga wasn't to be put off by such trifling details. Once she had her mind set on something there was no stopping her. 'I only said I would think of A PLAN,' she remarked. 'I didn't say anything about doing it. I mean, I would if I could, but I can't, so I won't, will I?'

It was the kind of remark to which there was really no reply, so while Olga settled down to think up her idea the others went their separate ways.

Matters became even more urgent over the next few days, for there were two more night raids on the Sawdust family's house. During the first some tufts were torn out of the dining-room carpet, and on the second occasion a packet of butter was left half-eaten on the kitchen table.

Unfortunately, Noel himself discovered the remains of the butter, and in doing so accidentally got some on to his own whiskers. He was caught in the act of licking them clean and from that moment on his fate was sealed. Threats which had been made more in fun than in anger suddenly became very real.

The only ray of hope was that Olga had actually seen the intruder leaving. Because it was dark at the time, she couldn't swear she'd recognized the shadowy figure as 'Stinker' Martin, but she could definitely say that it hadn't been Noel, simply by the sound of its voice.

In trying to leave as quietly as possible it had stepped on something sharp. There had been a muffled meeeow and then it had disappeared into the night, leaving Olga wide awake and with the first glimmerings of an idea forming in her mind.

The next morning she called an urgent meeting with Fangio and Graham.

As soon as they'd settled down she asked her first question.

'What,' she asked, 'would you think is the most sensitive part of a cat?

'I know it's not an easy question,' she said, as the others tried their best to think of an answer. 'I mean, it's hard to picture them having *any* sensitive parts at all . . .'

'Their whiskers?' hazarded Graham. Not having any whiskers himself he'd always imagined there must be something rather special about them, particularly as Noel seemed to spend so much time keeping his own in order.

Olga clucked impatiently. 'They only use those for going through holes,' she said. 'They haven't got much sense so they need something to tell them how wide they are. There's nothing sensitive about a cat's whiskers.'

'I'd rather you told us about your PLAN,' grumbled Fangio.

With an effort Olga brought herself back down to earth.

'All right,' she agreed reluctantly. 'Well, it isn't their whiskers that's the most sensitive part . . . it's their paws!' And she went on to explain all that had happened the previous night.

'The thing is,' she said at last, 'suppose we wait until after it gets dark and the Sawdust people have gone to bed, and then put something sharp on the *other* side of the pussy-flap? As soon as "Stinker" Martin climbs through he'll step on it and kick up such a din he'll wake everyone up and they'll come down and catch him!'

Olga sat back feeling very pleased with herself. It was a masterly PLAN. A plan to end all plans. One that couldn't possibly fail.

'Something sharp?' said Fangio at last. 'What sort of sharp?'

Olga gave a sigh.

'I don't know,' she said impatiently. 'Glass . . . Sawdust people put broken glass on top of walls to stop other people climbing over. I've seen it.'

'Oh, I've got masses of broken glass,' said Fangio sarcastically. 'I mean, I carry it around with me all the time. Besides, he might not tread on any of the sharp bits. If broken glass was any good we hedgehogs would have had it years ago. Why do you think we're

born with spikes on our backs? It's to protect ourselves. When anything tries to attack us we just roll
ourselves up into a ball. Why, just one prick of a
hedgehog's spike is enough to . . .'

Fangio broke off. He was about to curl himself up
in order to show the others exactly what he meant

when he suddenly realized they were hanging on his
every word.

'No,' he said firmly, looking from one to the
other, 'I'm *not* being trodden on by "Stinker"
Martin.'

'It's only *one* tread,' said Olga. 'Besides, if you
don't they may get rid of Noel. Just think what that
would mean. If they get rid of him there won't be

anyone to chase the birds away. And if there are lots of birds there won't be any insects left. You won't like that.'

Fangio stared up at Noel's pussy-flap. 'It's much too high,' he announced. 'I'd never reach it.'

'You would,' said Olga slowly, 'if you stood on Graham's back!'

If Olga had announced that the world was about to collapse beneath them her words could scarcely have had a greater effect on her audience. But she wouldn't listen to any arguments. The more reasons Fangio and Graham thought up as to why they should have nothing to do with HER PLAN, the more reasons she thought up as to why they should.

Even the Sawdust family noticed.

'I can't understand it,' said Mrs Sawdust as they went to bed that night. 'Fangio and Graham haven't left Olga's hutch all day. They were still there when I locked up. They kept peering up at Noel's pussy-flap. Anyone would think there was something "going on".'

'There'll be something going *out* tonight, if we have any more trouble,' said Mr Sawdust grimly. 'And it'll be spelt N . . . O . . . E . . . L!'

'Perhaps putting him out early will help?' said

Mrs Sawdust hopefully. 'He may come back so tired he'll go straight to sleep.'

'That,' said Mr Sawdust ominously, 'remains to be seen.'

Noel had been sent out soon after tea that evening, and his several attempts at returning home had been rebuffed by some very firm 'shoo's' from the rest of the family, so that in the end he'd gone off in a huff, leaving them all feeling slightly guilty.

'I do hope he hasn't taken it too badly,' said Mrs Sawdust. 'I mean, I'd hate him to think he really wasn't wanted.'

But the only reply she got from Mr Sawdust was a grunt as he turned out the light. Mr Sawdust had other things on his mind, but even so it was safe to say that none of them came anywhere near picturing what was happening one floor below. If they had he would have been out of bed like a shot.

The fact of the matter was, Olga, Fangio and Graham were having trouble. Or rather, to be more exact, Fangio was having trouble, and neither Olga nor Graham could do a thing about it.

Olga's plan had run up against an unexpected snag. The first part had gone well enough. After a certain amount of effort Fangio had managed to clamber on top of Graham's back, and from there he'd worked his way up to the hole in the door. It was then that the trouble had started. Noel's pussy-flap was made in such a way that it hinged from the inside. This meant that although it was easy to enter the house, anyone trying to back out again – especially anyone with prickles – tended to force the flap shut again.

Somehow, in trying to squeeze through the hole, Fangio had got himself well and truly jammed, so that he could neither climb back out again, nor, with

his back legs off the ground, could he push himself through into the house.

'I'm stuck!' he wailed, for what seemed like the fiftieth time. 'Help! Help! *Do* something!'

Olga tried another approach.

'I shouldn't be too long if I were you,' she called. 'I don't know, but I think I can hear "Stinker" coming!' And she lifted up her head and uttered a loud 'WheeeeeeooooooooooooooW'.

In normal circumstances even Olga would have had to admit that it wasn't very much like a cat, but it had the desired effect.

Fangio, his back legs working away like pistons, made one last desperate bid to free himself. There was a hurried scratching sound, followed by a loud metallic bang and a dull thud, and then silence.

'I hope he landed the right way up,' said Graham.

'If he's so good at rolling himself into a ball,' said Olga, 'I'm sure he can do a simple thing like turning himself over. He's not like a tortoise.

'Anyway,' she added, 'I've done my bit. I can't do any more. All we can do now is wait for "Stinker" to come.'

Graham cast an anxious glance over his shoulder. 'You can wait if you like,' he said. 'I'm going. I've done my bit too!' And without more ado he vanished into the darkness of the shrubbery.

Olga lay back in the hay and closed her eyes. She felt quite worn out from the strain of wondering whether or not Fangio would get through Noel's pussy-flap, and in no time at all she was fast asleep.

She woke suddenly to the sound of a tremendous howl. It was a howl fit to waken the dead, let alone a sleeping guinea-pig.

It went on and on and on.

It certainly woke the Sawdust family. Lights started coming on; there was the sound of running feet; and then voices – half-cross, half-scared, half-disbelieving – began to reach her ears.

Olga felt a glow of satisfaction. At last all her hard work was beginning to bear fruit. Now the Sawdust family would surely see the truth of the matter.

The back door opened and Mr Sawdust, wearing a dressing-gown and looking strangely ruffled, stood framed in the opening for a moment while he went down and placed something on the ground.

'"Stinker" Martin!' exclaimed Fangio bitterly, as the door slammed shut behind him. '"*Stinker" Martin*!'

For the first time that night a doubt entered Olga's mind. 'Is something the matter?' she asked.

'I'll say,' said Fangio. 'It wasn't "Stinker" Martin at all. It was Noel! You forgot to tell him about your plan. He came back home and landed right on top of me. Now his feet are full of my prickles and he's got to go off to the vet again in the morning. There's a terrible rumpus going on.'

'Well,' said Olga, recovering her composure, 'at least we know my PLAN works. Perhaps we shall be luckier next time.'

'Next time?' exclaimed Fangio. '*Next time*! There won't be a next time. Not for me there won't. And if you think I'm fed up, you wait till you see Noel!'

Olga gave a sigh as Fangio stalked off. When she thought of the amount of effort she put into helping others . . . and for what? Really, there was no gratitude left in the world. She decided she would go back to sleep at once and let them get on with it.

It was some two days before Olga saw Noel again, and when he did return from the vet, nursing two heavily bandaged front paws, he was strangely subdued.

He hobbled up to Olga's house and peered up at her.

'Er . . . thanks,' he said gruffly.

If Olga was taken aback she tried her best not to show it. 'That's all right,' she said.

'I still don't see how you knew,' said Noel.

'Well, er, Wheeeeeeeeeeeee,' said Olga, playing for time, 'guinea-pigs are like that. They do know about things.'

'I mean,' said Noel, half talking to himself, 'with me at the vet's it had to be someone else, didn't it? I mean, when "Stinker" Martin broke in next night and I wasn't there they knew it must have been him all the time.'

Olga stared at Noel open-mouthed. It was the first she'd heard of another break-in, though now he mentioned it something had woken her up during the night, but at the time it had seemed like rain.

'I shouldn't think *he'll* be coming back again,' said Noel in tones of satisfaction. 'I hear Mr Sawdust threw a bucket of water over him. Was he very wet?'

'Well,' said Olga, feeling unusually truthful for once. 'I must admit I didn't actually see it.

'But I heard it,' she added hastily, seeing the look of disappointment on Noel's face. 'It woke me up with a terrible splash.

'The thing is,' she said, 'drawing up PLANS is *very* tiring work. Especially PLANS that work out right in the end. I'm afraid I was so worn out I went straight back to sleep again.'

CHAPTER NINE

The Day the Guinea-pigs
Learned to Sing

One morning Olga da Polga woke feeling unusually
cold. Overnight there had been a change in the
weather and when she peered through her bedroom
window her breath froze to the glass, making it hard
to see out.

The cold snap seemed to have taken everyone by

surprise. In the distance she could see the vague forms of Fangio and Graham making hasty preparations for their winter homes, and even Noel looked as if he was having second thoughts about taking his morning stroll. He was walking very gingerly indeed along the frost-covered path, placing each back paw neatly into the spot left by his front ones as he picked his way down the garden in order to survey his property.

Although Noel tolerated the other animals in the household – and he could hardly do otherwise – he regarded the Sawdust family's garden as being very much 'his' territory, and he was always most offended if he caught sight of any squirrels or birds daring to make use of it.

The Sawdust family obviously hadn't expected a change in the weather either, for the wooden panel over Olga's front door had been left off. During the winter months Olga always had a panel over her wire mesh at night, and although it made the mornings dark she was very grateful, for it kept out the worst of the bad weather.

Olga couldn't make up her mind whether to stay snuggled up in her warm nest of hay for a while or venture out into the cold dining-room in search of some oats. In the end she decided on some oats. She was a great believer in having plenty of food inside her when the weather turned cold. There was nothing like it for warmth.

But Olga had another surprise coming her way. Having scraped out the last of the bowl, she was backing away in order to chew the oats more thoroughly when she suddenly let out a loud cry.

'WheeeeeeeeeeEEEEEEEEEEEEEEEEE!'

She had been so taken up with her breakfast she hadn't noticed her water bowl right behind her. She

sat down in it by mistake and then jumped up again twice as quickly as it was very, very cold.

When she looked round she discovered why. The water was completely frozen over!

Her dignity ruffled, Olga gave a shiver and hurried back into her bedroom, burying herself deep inside the warm hay again, leaving only a tiny peephole so that she could watch the goings-on outside in comfort.

Shortly afterwards Karen Sawdust, dressed in coat and scarf, came out to give Olga's dining-room its morning clean. Olga was pleased to see that when she went off to fetch the breakfast she took the water bowl with her so that she could melt the ice. During the summer Olga was able to get most of the moisture she needed from the grass and other greenstuff she ate, but in winter, when she lived mainly on oats, she relied on her water bowl.

As soon as she was on her own again she hurried out for a drink. The water tasted warm and very pleasant, and it made her feel a lot better.

Some while later, after she'd had her own breakfast, Karen Sawdust reappeared. This time she was carrying a small black case, and in her other hand she had a silver object on the end of a long wire.

She seemed to be talking to it. Olga distinctly heard her as she went past.

'One, two, three,' she said. 'One, two, three . . . testing.'

She went down the garden, still carrying the object in her hand, and Olga watched with interest as she held it towards Noel, almost as if she expected him to eat it. But Noel gave it a very disdainful glance, and after a brief sniff he looked the other way, pretending he was only interested in washing himself.

Next, Karen Sawdust tried pointing it towards some birds sitting up in a nearby tree, safely out of Noel's reach.

For some reason or other this didn't seem to satisfy her either, so she approched Fangio and Graham – but they took even less notice.

'Whatever's going on?' thought Olga, as Karen Sawdust drew near, for she could see she looked most disappointed. 'What *can* she want?'

'Hullo, Olga,' said Karen Sawdust, as she opened the front door and thrust the object towards the bedroom. 'Come on, say something. Whee! Whee! Whee!'

But Olga refused to play. The fact of the matter was that although she trusted Karen Sawdust and

didn't think for one moment that she would do her any harm, she wasn't all that keen on having things pointed at her without warning. She gave a sniff, and she agreed with Noel – it wasn't really worth bothering about. The silver object had a most uninteresting smell – if it could be called any sort of smell at all, and she decide she didn't wish to know about it.

'I don't know,' said Karen Sawdust as Mrs Sawdust came into the garden, 'any other time Olga would be squeaking her head off, but when you really want her to say something there isn't as much as a peep.'

'Perhaps you should have disguised the microphone as a carrot,' said her mother. 'You might have got her to sing for her breakfast then. Anyway, is it *that* important?'

'It certainly is,' exclaimed Karen Sawdust. 'It's a school project. I'm supposed to get all these animal voices by the end of the week . . .'

Olga's ears pricked up. 'Animal voices! By the end of the wheeek! Why ever hadn't she said? If I'd known she wanted some *voices* I could have done lots.' And she let out a loud 'Wheeeeeeeeee!' just to show how good she was at it. The noise that came out wasn't quite as piercing as the one she'd done earlier when she sat on the ice, but it was very nearly as loud.

However, it came too late. By then Karen and Mrs Sawdust had gone inside, the kitchen door had closed, and there was no one left to hear her effort.

'What's going on?' asked Noel as he drew near. 'What was that awful screech just now?'

'Awful screech!' exclaimed Olga. '*Awful screech*! I was making a special "voice" for Karen Sawdust.

'It's a project,' she continued knowledgeably. 'A school project.'

'A project?' repeated Noel. 'What's a project?'

'It's when you collect lots of different voices by the end of the week,' said Olga, 'and put them all into a case. You start with the worst first and end up with the best. I expect that's why she saved me until last.'

Noel, who'd been about to disappear through his

pussy-flap, paused and looked back at Olga in dis-
belief.

'Haven't you ever wondered how guinea-pigs
came to have such lovely voices?' asked Olga inno-
cently.

Noel let the pussy-flap fall back into place. 'No,' he
said, 'I haven't!'

Olga settled back, for she could feel a story coming
on.

'Guinea-pigs,' she said loudly, as she caught sight
of Fangio and Graham coming along the path, 'have
the most lovely singing voices.

'When the world began,' she went on, warming to
her tale as the others gathered round, 'no one could
sing. You see, it had never been thought of. All anyone had done until then was make grunting noises.
Apart from a few cats who could meeow,' she added
grudgingly for Noel's benefit. 'But no one thought
very much of *that* as a sound.

'And then one day a guinea-pig made an important
discovery. He found that if he put his head inside
his feeding bowl and make a noise it sounded deeper
than usual.'

Olga looked round for her own bowl. 'I'll show
you if you like,' she said.

The effect of squeaking into an empty feeding bowl was something Olga had noticed quite early on in her life. She had also learned that squeaking into a full bowl made no difference whatever to her voice, and she suddenly realized she hadn't even touched her breakfast that morning. So instead of saying anything she just stood over her bowl for a moment or two with her eyes closed and her mouth wide open.

The others listened in silence until Olga opened her eyes again.

'Did you like it?' she asked.

'Er, yes,' said Noel grudgingly. 'It wasn't bad.'

'I've heard worse,' agreed Fangio.

'I didn't hear anything,' said Graham bluntly.

'You need very good earsight,' said Olga. 'The deeper the sound the harder it is to hear.

'Anyway, the guinea-pig who first made the discovery told his friends, and soon they were all doing it. They found the bigger the bowl the better it sounded. Then they had an idea. They dug a hole in the ground, making the sides smooth and hard, and when they'd finished they all climbed inside and tried again. This time the noise was so loud and deep it could be heard for miles around. In fact, they found that the deeper they went down into the earth the more the other animals liked it.'

' *That* I can believe,' said Noel.

Olga ignored the remark. 'If you've never heard a massed choir of guinea-pigs singing deep notes,' she said, 'you haven't lived.

'Anyway, the same guinea-pig had yet another idea. Suppose, instead of digging deeper and deeper into the ground, they tried going the other way? Suppose they went up instead of down – what would happen then?

'He gathered all his friends together to explain his plan, and after a lot of discussion they set off towards a distant mountain. Because it was a long way away they had to take lots of things with them for the journey. Some of them carried bundles of dandelion leaves on their backs; others were in charge of the carrots. Some had hay and straw for the bedding at nights; others pushed bowls of water and oats along the ground.

'The news of their great adventure spread, and as they got higher and higher up the mountain all the other animals in the land came to watch. Soon the fields below were full of cows and sheep and cats and dogs and tortoises and hedgehogs.

'In fact,' said Olga, who was beginning to run out of ideas, 'all the animals you could possibly think of.'

'Mountains have snow on them,' said Noel suspiciously. 'I've seen pictures.'

But Olga wasn't to be put off. 'That was the hardest part of all,' she said. 'The higher they went, the snowier it became. So they took it in turns to sit in

their bowls. Some sat inside while the others pushed, and when the ones who were doing the pushing got tired they changed over.

'They were very *big* bowls,' she added firmly, before there were any more interruptions, 'because it was a *very* long journey. And because it was a long journey, there was hardly any food left.

'When they reached the top of the mountain they found to their surprise that it was hollow and shaped just like a very large bowl. There was a lake inside the hollow and it had frozen over.

'They rested on the bank for a while and then, when they had got their breath back, they kept it all inside themselves and gathered together in the middle of the lake.

'Then at a signal from the leader they all sat down, opened their mouths, and let out a cry.

'It was the loudest and highest sound that had ever been heard. It was so loud and high and big it rolled all the way down the mountain, across the valley, up the other side, and then fell off the world.

'You can still hear it sometimes,' said Olga, 'when the wind blows it in the right direction.

'When the guinea-pigs came back down the other animals tried to find out the secret of how they had managed to sing such high notes, but they wouldn't tell. They kept it a secret and it's been a secret until this very day.

'In fact,' said Olga, putting on one of her superior looks, 'I'm the only one left in the world who knows it!'

Olga's audience looked suitably impressed.

'Come on,' said Noel. 'You can tell *us*.'

Olga hesitated. Like all good storytellers she knew exactly how to keep her listeners on tenterhooks.

'It was all to do with the lake being frozen over,' she said at last. 'When the guinea-pigs sat down it was so cold they all jumped up again and did what anyone else would have done. They went 'Wheeeee-eeeeeee!' at the tops of their voices.

'I'll show you what I mean, if you like,' Olga backed towards her water bowl. 'But I should put your paws over your ears, because it's very, very loud.'

Closing her eyes again, she took a deep breath and sat down ready to give the loudest squeak she'd ever done in her life.

But all she managed was 'WheeeeeeEEEEuggghhh-hhhhhhhhhhhhh!'

'Was that it?' asked Noel in disgust. 'Wheeeeee-EEEEuggghhhhhhhhhhhh!'

'It sounded more like a rusty hinge on a wet day to me,' said Fangio. 'There's one down the bottom of the garden. It sounded just like that.'

'I'm going,' said Graham. He gazed anxiously at the leaden sky. 'Tomorrow's another year and I don't want to get caught without a bed for the winter.'

'Wait for me!' called Fangio.

'Good-bye!' said Noel.

Olga watched the others as they went their separate ways. It had been a good story, one of her very best, right up until the end. But the end had been like a damp squib.

And now that was how her end felt – very damp. For in her excitement she had completely forgotten that Karen Sawdust had changed her water and it was no longer frozen over.

'Wheeeeeuggggghhhhhh!' she said to the world in general. 'Wheeeeeugggggghhhhhhhh!'

It wasn't a deep squeak, and it certainly wasn't a low one; it was a *damp* squeak, and it summed up her feelings to the full.

Had she been around to hear it, Karen Sawdust might well have wanted to add it to her collection, but she wasn't, and so it was lost for all time.

Olga glanced out at the weather. It looked as she felt – cold, and rather downcast.

Taking a deep breath she gave yet another squeak; but this time it had a much more decided note to it.

'Wheeeeeeeeup!' it went. 'I don't really see why I should be the only one round here to suffer. It's high time I emigrated too!'

With that she disappeared into her bedroom, closed her eyes very firmly, and didn't come out again until she was thoroughly dry and ready for her supper.

By the time that was over and her house had been cleaned out for the night, she felt much, much better. In fact, all in all, she was back to being her normal self again.

Really and truly, she decided, there was nothing like a full stomach and a warm house for making everything seem right in the world – especially when you were a guinea-pig, tired out through telling lots of tales.